Dot has a cat.

The cat is Mit.

Dot and Mit

by Bobby Lynn Maslen
pictures by John R. Maslen

Scholastic Inc.
New York • Toronto • London • Auckland • Sydney • Mexico City • New Delhi • Hong Kong • Buenos Aires

Beginning sounds for Book 5:

N n – nut

P p – pencil

I i – inchworm

Ask for Bob Books at your local bookstore, or visit www.bobbooks.com.

No part of this publication may be reproduced, stored in a retrieval system, or transmitted in any form or by any means, electronic, mechanical, photocopying, recording, or otherwise, without written permission of the publisher. For information regarding permission, write to Scholastic Inc., Attention: Permissions Department, 557 Broadway, New York, NY 10012.

ISBN 0-545-02718-7

6 5 4 3 2 1   7 8 9 10 11/0

Printed in China
This edition first printing, September 2007

Dot and Mit sit on a mat.

Dot is hot. Mit is hot.

Dot did nap.

Mit did not nap.

"Sit, Dot."

Dot did not nap.

The End

Available Bob Books®:

Set 1: Beginning Readers — With consistent new sounds added gradually, your new reader is gently introduced to all the letters of the alphabet. They can soon say, "I read the whole book!®"

Set 2: Advancing Beginners — The use of three-letter words and consistent vowel sounds in slightly longer stories build skill and confidence.

Set 3: Word Families — Consonant blends, endings and a few sight words advance reading skills while the use of word families keep reading manageable.

Set 4: Compound Words — Longer books and complex words engage young readers as proficiency advances.

Set 5: Long Vowels — Silent *e* and other vowel blends build young readers' vocabulary and aptitude.

Bob Books® Collections:

Collection 1 — Includes Set 1: Beginning Readers and part of Set 2: Advancing Beginners

Collection 2 — Includes part of Set 2: Advancing Beginners and Set 3: Word Families

Collection 3 — Includes Set 4: Compound Words and Set 5: Long Vowels